# Mermaid Seal

## a selkie tale

Written by
Consie Berghausen &
Chloe Berghausen

Illustrated by
Nina Berghausen

Published and Distributed by RICHER Press

Cover Design: Nina Berghausen

Illustrations: Nina Berghausen

Library of Congress Control Number: 2021936246

Consie Berghausen and Chloe Berghausen

Mermaid Seal: A Selkie Seal
1st   edition

1. Children 2. Education 3. Reference

ISBN 13: 978-1-7335693-5-4 (Paperback)
ISBN 13: 978-1-7335693-6-1 (Hardback)


May 2021

Printed in the United States of America

# Parent's Corner

1. Cape Cod has Harbor and Grey seals

2. Harbor seals are small, no longer than 5 feet

3. Grey seals are bigger, with males up to 8 feet

4. Grey seals are sometimes called horse heads because of their long snouts

5. While seal watching stay at least 50 yards away

6. Selkie Seal comes from Norse and Celtic mythology ("selkie fowk" means seal folk)

7. According to this mythology, Selkie seals are usually females who transform into humans when they remove their coat

8. The words Selkie, mermaid, and seal maiden are interchangeable

# Eye Spy

Crab | Book | Row Boat | Balloon | Goggles | Seagull |

Sailboat | Sand Dollar | Whale | Baseball | Octopus |

Umbrella | Bicycle | Oysters | Lighthouse | Fishing Pole |

Dog | Ice Cream Truck | Sea Turtle | Jellyfish

Cape Cod seals frolic on outer beaches
Their barks make music with seabird screeches
Clear shallow waters grace miles of sand
A haven called home, expansive and grand

Harbor and grey seals both live together
Swimming and playing in all kinds of weather
They rest and roll on the sunny beach shore
With so many friends it is fun galore

One type of creature that is sure danger
The great white shark is no Cape Cod stranger
Cruising in the sea and near to the shore
Hiding and hunting in this sea creature war

One type of seal has a special power
She can leave the sea and her fins for hours
Or days depending on the situation
A shocking seal to person transformation

Some call her a mermaid or Selkie seal
Some say she's a myth, but she's very real

This Selkie seal can swim in the ocean
Or walk on the beach by changing her motion
Losing her fur coat is where the magic begins
Having legs and arms, and not tail or fins

Her magic is old but the girl is new
She's rescued seals, but can save people too
It's a sunny day, no one is around
Time to leave water and walk on the ground
Now Selkie seal swims up onto sea grass
Hiding in reeds while nearby cars pass
She folds her fur coat and tucks it away
Stretches her legs and hears someone say,

"Hey!" A boy in the dunes can't believe his eyes
A seal, now a girl is quite a surprise

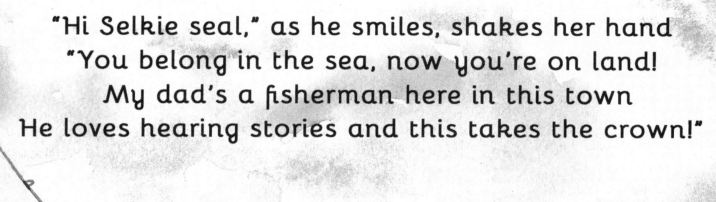

"Hi Selkie seal," as he smiles, shakes her hand
"You belong in the sea, now you're on land!
My dad's a fisherman here in this town
He loves hearing stories and this takes the crown!"

"Will you show me your world here on the land?"
"I'd like to see yours, in the sea not on sand"
"Let's go to town and stroll on the streets
There is fun to be had and people to meet"

Walking along the charming old streets
He stops and asks "What do you like to eat?"

"Sushi and seaweed, crab legs are a treat"
Selkie seal laughed, and He said "That's neat"

"I like ice cream, fudge, well...mostly dessert
Chowder and salad have to come first"

She had never eaten something so sweet
Ice cream dripped as they walked down the street

He laughed at the mess, said "Let's clean you up!"
Next to the library there was a pup
It lapped at her hands with many a squeal
She gasped, her hands clean, "Is this a land seal?"
"Let's go inside, walk around, find a book
So many choices, it's fun to just look!"

Toys, books, balloons, and eating ice cream
This little Cape town seemed a wonderful dream

"Listen to the beautiful church bell chimes
Do you know what that means? It's bandstand time!"

The bandstand swelled with the beginning song
They play every Friday all summer long
Amazed and grateful for her lucky day
Selkie seal promised tomorrow to play
Under the sea and to show him her life
They sat, watched the sunset, and said goodnight

They planned to meet early at Oyster Pond
With few waves and soft sand, a place of calm
Ready to teach, she smiled in delight
Excited to show him her ocean life

"Hold on to me, breathe the air in my fur
Are you ready to go?" "I am for sure"
She dove straight down to begin their fun ride
He felt the pull of the current and tide

The underwater world is quite a sight
Bluefish, oysters, and crabs, what a delight!
Gurgles, bubbles, and a whale's distant song
This world is so cool, it's where she belongs

They swam by the Vineyard and Nantucket
Where clammers fill up their metal buckets

And beach kids play with shovels and buckets

Clinging together they take a deep dive
Below is the ship lying now on its side
He wonders if there is treasure inside
As they get closer he quickly decides
He releases his hold on Selkie seal
And wiggles through a hole, slim like an eel
It's dark inside, there's no light to see
No way to find where the treasure might be

Scared of the dark and he's run out of air
She sees the danger and is quickly aware

He needs her help, she races through the hole
To grab him, give him air, that is her goal

He gasps "Sorry, I just wanted to know
About the secrets and treasures below"
Selkie seal smiles,
she's curious too
"I promise to save you,
that's what friends do!"

Safely together they turn to go home
He holds on tightly, not wanting to roam

Past islands and beaches riding the waves
Swimming with sea creatures, oh what a day!

They land on the beach, lit up by the moon
Big smiles and promises to meet up soon

His world her world, shared in just two days
A magical friendship, wouldn't you say?

# The Team: Consie, Chloe, and Nina Berghausen

• Consie is the author of five other books. She splits her time between Tucson, Arizona and Chatham, Massachusetts.

• Chloe is Consie's daughter and writing partner. She is a keen reader and spends her free time collecting plants and showering her 3 cats with love.

• Nina is also her daughter and a graphic design artist. She has a great sense of humor and is a huge animal lover.

Mermaid Seal
*a selkie tale*

Written by
Consie Berghausen &
Chloe Berghausen

Illustrated by
Nina Berghausen

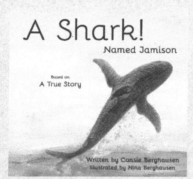

A Shark!
Named Jamison

Based on
A True Story

Written by Consie Berghausen
Illustrated by Nina Berghausen

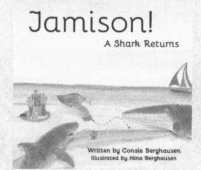

Jamison!
A Shark Returns

Written by Consie Berghausen
Illustrated by Nina Berghausen

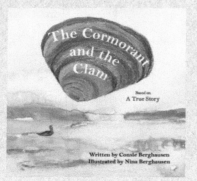

The Cormorant and the Clam

Based on
A True Story

Written by Consie Berghausen
Illustrated by Nina Berghausen

The Sonoran Desert,
A Magical Place

Written by Consie Berghausen
Illustrated by Nina Berghausen

The Saltwater Marsh,
A Magical Place

Written by Consie Berghausen
Illustrated by Nina Berghausen

Website: consieberghausen.com
Facebook: facebook.com/consieandninaberghausen
Email: 22consie@gmail.com

CPSIA information can be obtained
at www.ICGtesting.com
Printed in the USA
JSHW012011130521
14714JS00002B/9

9 781733 569354